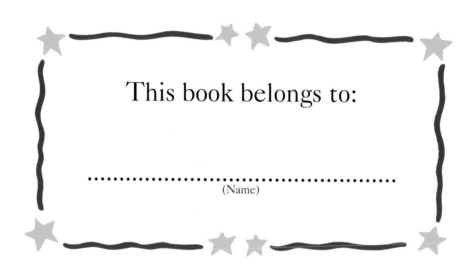

This book belongs to:

....
(Name)

The Sandman

Illustrated by Judy Deykin

$\mathcal{F}$ar, far away, high up in the sky, the Sandman lives on a fluffy, white cloud. During the day, when all the people down on the earth are awake, the Sandman is asleep. And at night, when everyone on earth is sleeping, the Sandman is awake.

The Sandman's best friend is the Moon. Every night as it starts getting dark, the Moon gently wakes the Sandman by whispering softly, "Wake up, Sandman! It's time to sprinkle sleep dust over all the little children!" Then the Sandman gets up, opens his umbrella, and floats down to the earth.

"Tonight I'll start with Anne," thought the Sandman one clear evening, and he glided down to her house. He landed on the kitchen window sill without a sound and peered into the room. Anne was sitting at the table, eating a sandwich and drinking hot chocolate.

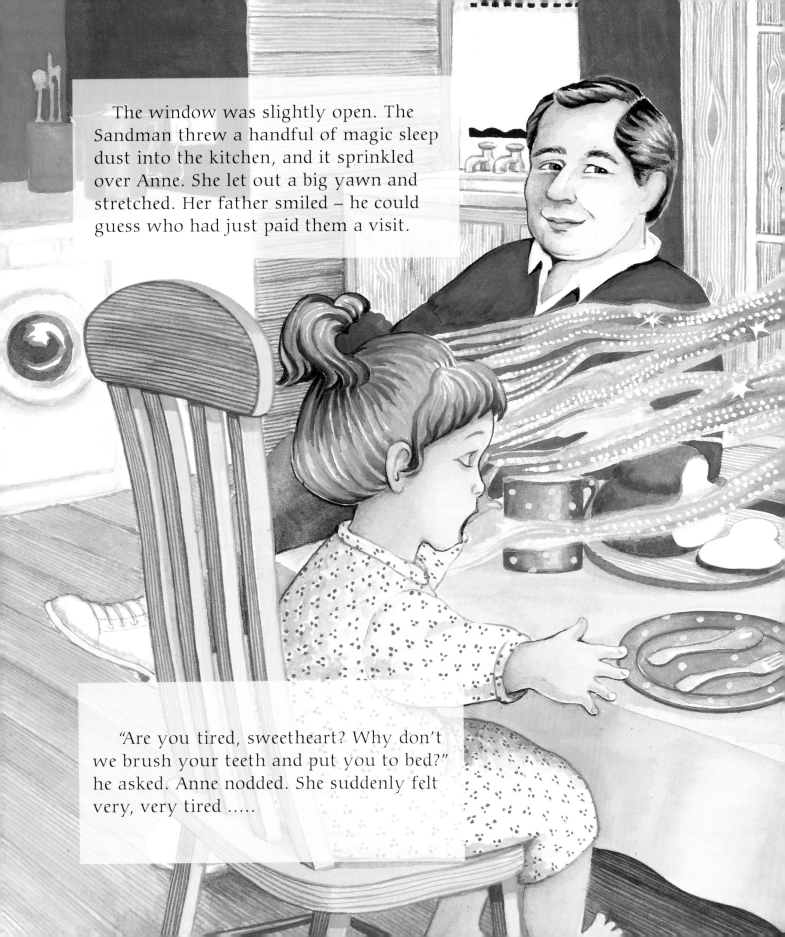

The window was slightly open. The Sandman threw a handful of magic sleep dust into the kitchen, and it sprinkled over Anne. She let out a big yawn and stretched. Her father smiled – he could guess who had just paid them a visit.

"Are you tired, sweetheart? Why don't we brush your teeth and put you to bed?" he asked. Anne nodded. She suddenly felt very, very tired .....

Anne's father lifted her up
in his arms and gently
carried her upstairs.

Anne brushed her teeth, and climbed in bed. By the time her father came to tuck her into bed, Anne had already fallen asleep!

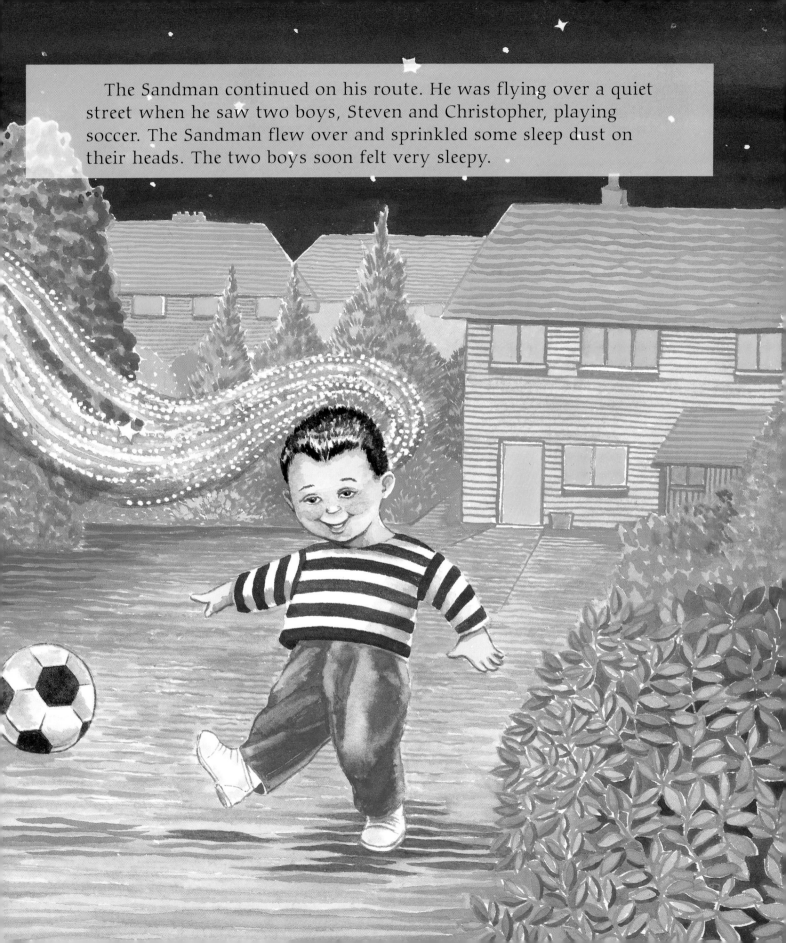

The Sandman continued on his route. He was flying over a quiet street when he saw two boys, Steven and Christopher, playing soccer. The Sandman flew over and sprinkled some sleep dust on their heads. The two boys soon felt very sleepy.

"I'm going home," said Steven. He walked toward the apartment building where he lived and called back to Christopher, "Let's play again tomorrow!"

In the meantime, the Sandman was flying over the apartment building sprinkling his magic sleep dust over all the other little children who lived there. All of the children in the building began to feel very tired.

Christopher went back to his house and took a nice, hot bath. He was getting sleepier and sleepier as he walked into his room.

He put on his pyjamas, put away his toys, and slid into bed. How warm and comfy it felt! Christopher soon drifted off to sleep.

At last the Sandman had visited all the little children on earth, and they slept sweetly in their beds. As the Sandman flew up towards his cloud, he passed Christopher's house. The Sandman smiled when he saw Christopher asleep in his bed.

The Sandman hummed his favorite lullaby as he flew. His best friend, the Moon, was waiting when he returned and together they watched over all the children sleeping far, far down below all night long.